So Many Me's

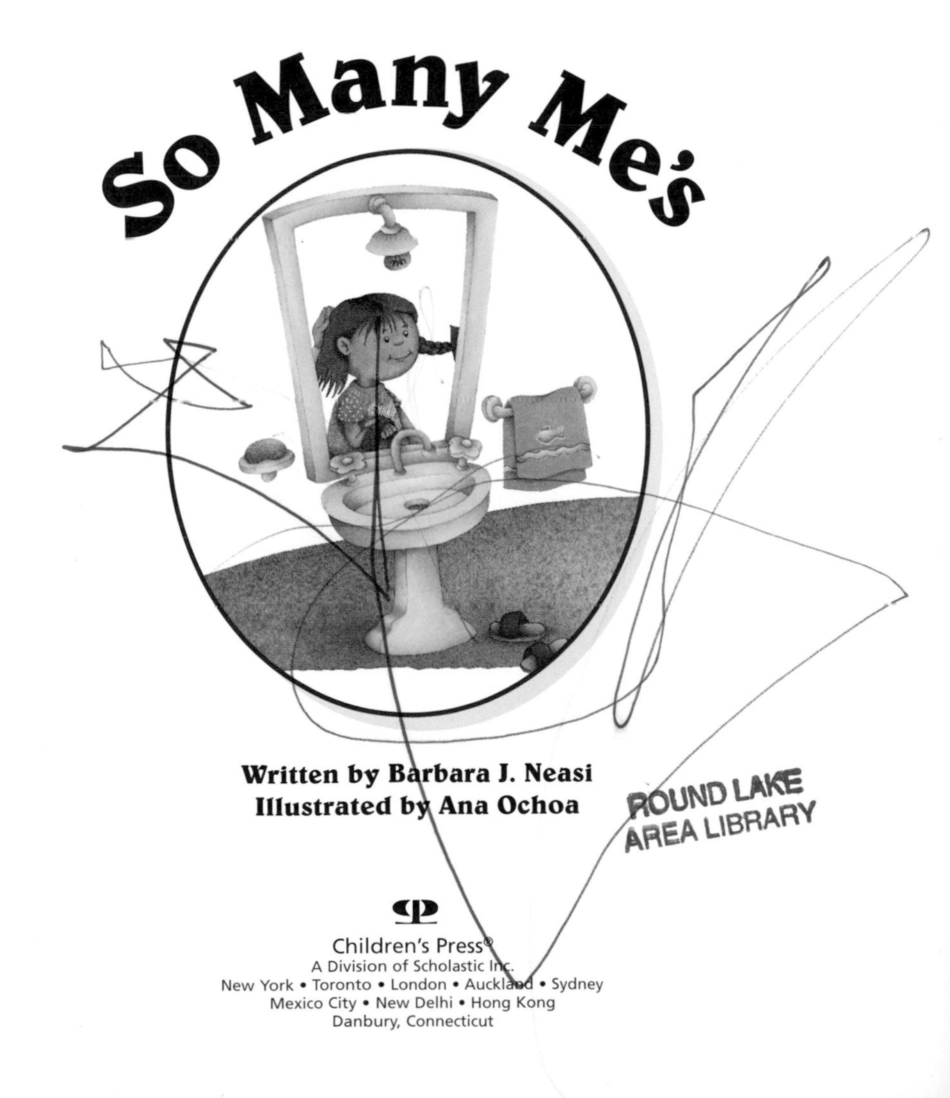

Written by Barbara J. Neasi
Illustrated by Ana Ochoa

Children's Press®
A Division of Scholastic Inc.
New York • Toronto • London • Auckland • Sydney
Mexico City • New Delhi • Hong Kong
Danbury, Connecticut

For Alexis, Dalton, and Jordin, the ultimate Imagination Kids
—B.J.N.

To Santiago, Patricio, and Anita
—A.O.

Reading Consultants

Linda Cornwell
Literacy Specialist

Katharine A. Kane
Education Consultant
(Retired, San Diego County Office of Education
and San Diego State University)

Library of Congress Cataloging-in-Publication Data

Neasi, Barbara J.
So many me's / written by Barbara J. Neasi ; illustrated
by Ana Ochoa.- 1st American ed.
p. cm. — (Rookie reader)
Summary: A girl contemplates the many different roles she plays in her family and community, including daughter, granddaughter, sister, cousin, student, patient, and friend.
ISBN 0-516-22883-8 (lib. bdg) 0-516-27786-3 (pbk.)
[1. Identity—Fiction.] I. Ochoa, Ana, ill. II. Title. III. Series.
PZ7.N295So 2003
[E]—dc21

2003003891

Printed in the United States of America.

1 2 3 4 5 6 7 8 9 10 R 12 11 10 09 08 07 06 05 04 03

Here I am!

How many me's do you see?

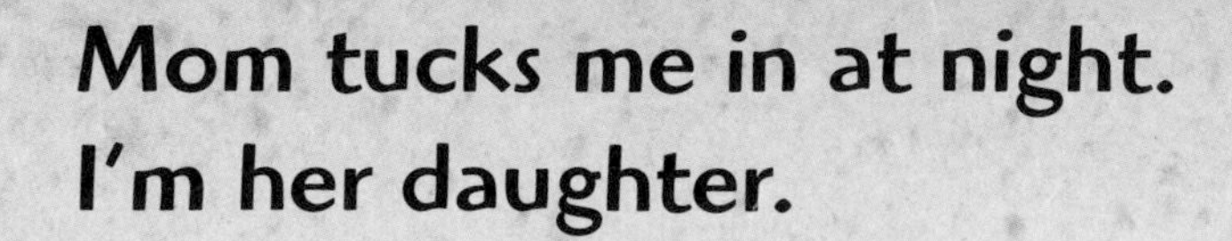

Mom tucks me in at night.
I'm her daughter.

Grandpa pushes me
in the wheelbarrow.
I'm his granddaughter.

I feed Baby William his bottle.
I'm his big sister.

Cathy braids my hair for school.
I'm her little sister.

Joan and Joe go camping
with me in the summer.
I'm their cousin.

4 + 6 =
7 + 2 =
3 + 5 = 8
1
2
3

Mrs. Brown teaches my class.
I'm her student.

Jane lives next door.
I'm her neighbor.

Michael and I are on
the same soccer team.
I'm his friend.

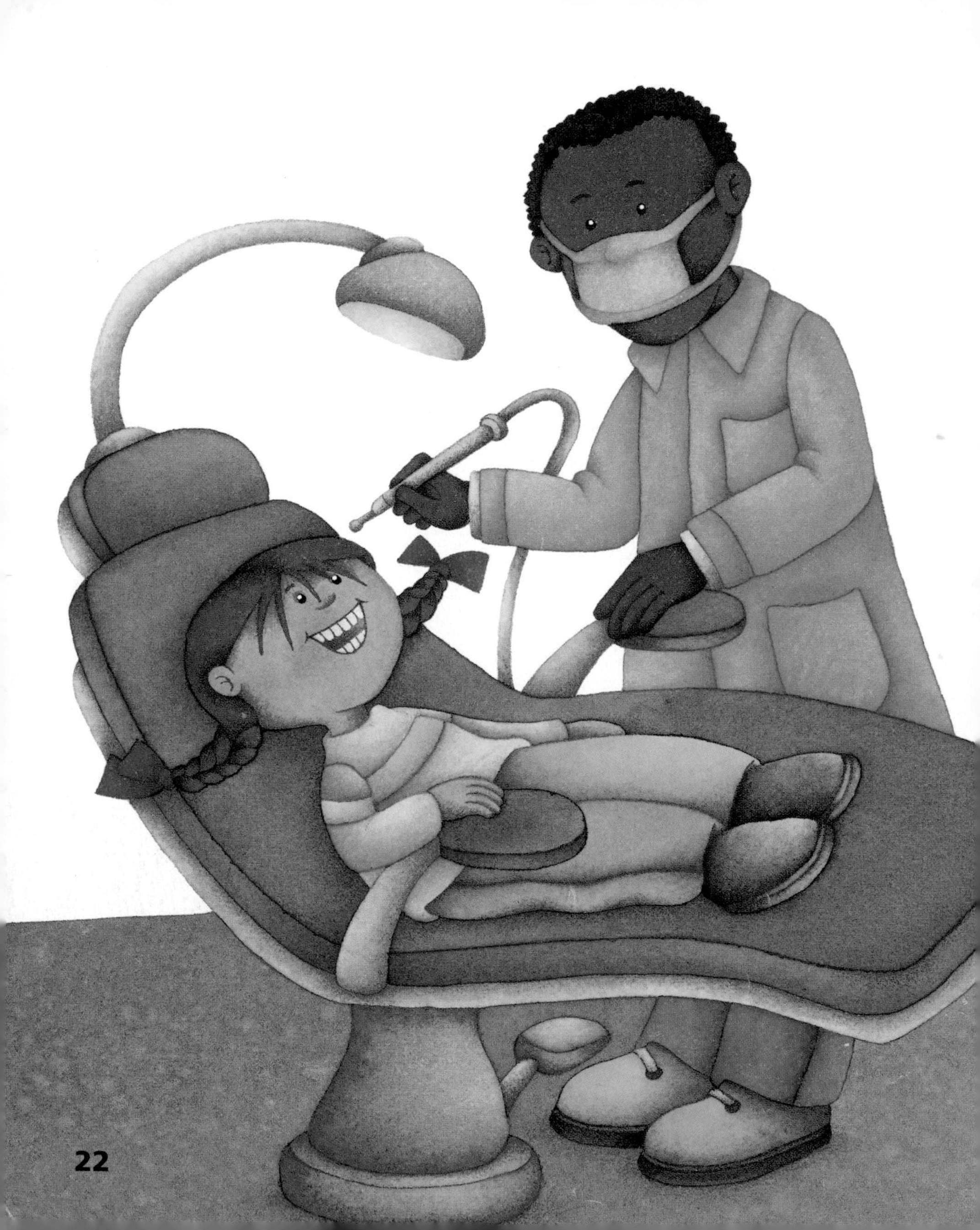

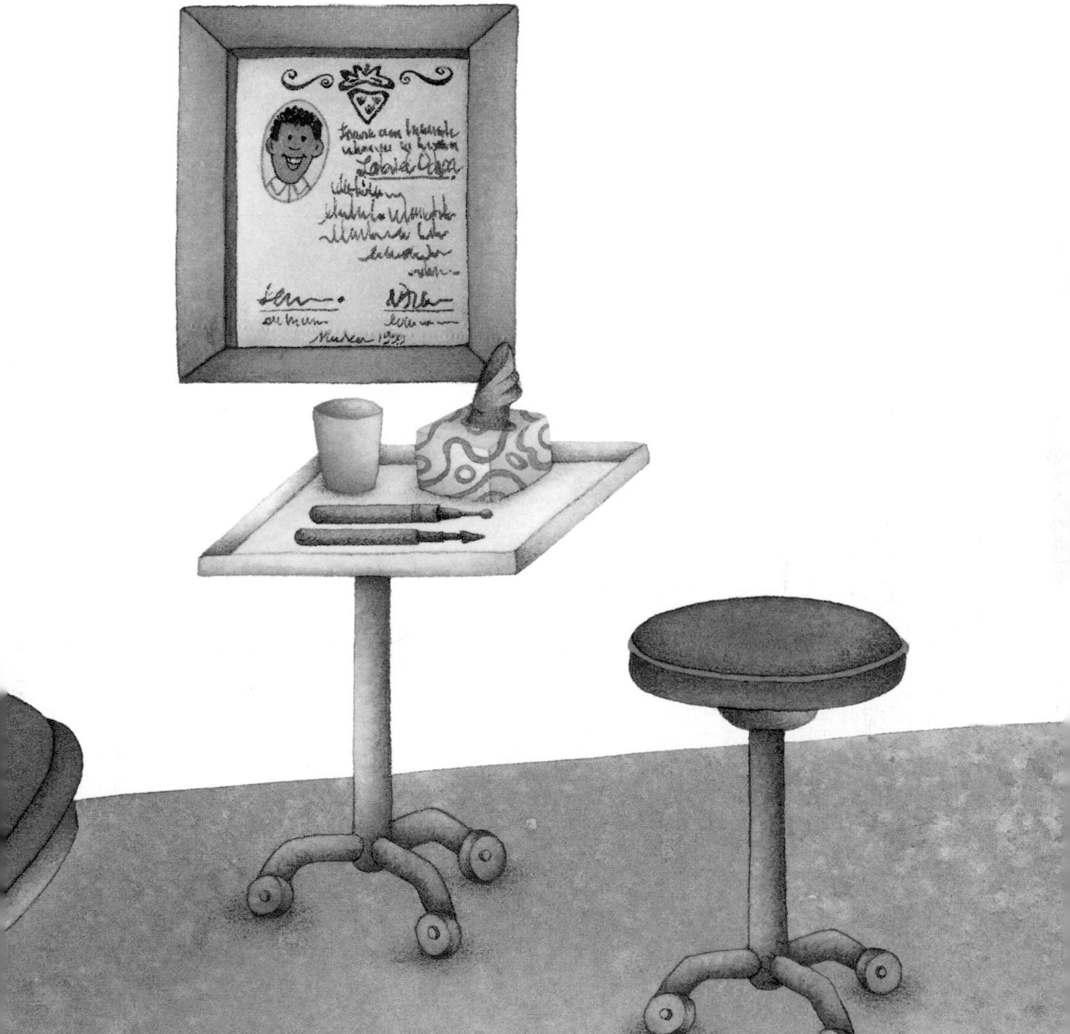

Dr. Wilson cleans my teeth.
I'm his patient.

When I dance on Daddy's feet,

he says I'm his princess.

I don't know. How can it be?

How can there be so many me's?

Word List (82 words)

am
and
are
at
baby
be
big
bottle
braids
Brown
camping
can
Cathy
class
cleans
cousin
Daddy's
dance
daughter
do
don't
door
Dr.
feed
feet
for
friend
go
grand-
daughter
Grandpa
hair
he
her
here
his
how
I
I'm
in
it
Jane
Joan
Joe
know
little
lives
many
me
me's
Michael
Mom
Mrs.
my
neighbor
next
night
on
patient
princess
pushes
same
says
school
see
sister
so
soccer
student
summer
teaches
team
teeth
the
their
there
tucks
wheelbarrow
when
William
Wilson
with
you

About the Author

Barbara J. Neasi is a children's writer and a substitute teacher. She lives in Moline, Illinois, with her husband, Randy, Tyson the dog, and Peanut the cat. They share a little gray house with a big garden, where her three grandchildren pick flowers and pumpkins, while squirrels, chipmunks, raccoons, and birds munch on crackers, seeds, and corn. She has also written *Just Like Me* in the *A Rookie Reader* series.

About the Illustrator

Ana Ochoa was born and raised in Mexico City. She has been in love with color and painting ever since she can remember. She painted everywhere she could, such as on her bedroom and classroom walls. Finally, she studied graphic design and discovered that she could keep on doing what she liked best for a living. Now, she is one of the lucky people living her dream and working to make kids happy.